Gowanus Dogs

Jonathan Frost

Frances Foster Books

Farrar, Straus and Giroux   New York

IN MEMORY OF MY FATHER, PAUL D. FROST

Copyright © 1999 by Jonathan Frost

All rights reserved

Distributed in Canada by Douglas & McIntyre Ltd.

Printed and bound in the United States of America by Berryville Graphics

Designed by Filomena Tuosto

First edition, 1999

Library of Congress Cataloging-in-Publication Data

Frost, Jonathan, 1949–

Gowanus dogs / Jonathan Frost. — 1st ed.

p.   cm.

"Frances Foster books."

Summary: A homeless man who lives under a bridge in Brooklyn finds his life changing when he decides to adopt a wild dog.

ISBN 0-374-31058-0

[1. Dogs—Fiction. 2. Homeless persons—Fiction. 3. Brooklyn (New York, N.Y.)—Fiction.] I. Title.

PZ7.F9206Go   1999

[Fic]—dc21   98-35523

A PUPPY WITH NO NAME woke up early in the morning. She made a high sound in her throat for her mother to hear. It meant "I'm awake, and I'm hungry."

The mother dog stretched and stood up. The puppy poked her two brothers with her nose to wake them, and the whole family went outside.

The puppies and their mother lived in a rusty mixing tank from an old cement truck, amid piles of rubble and huge chunks of cast-off concrete.

Next door at the South Brooklyn Concrete Company, a crane was unloading sand and stone from a barge on the Gowanus Canal.

The mother dog led her puppies up and over the hill.

They looked and sniffed, sniffed and looked everywhere for food. At last they came to a street where it was trash-collection day—the best day of the week for hungry wild dogs in the city. All along the sidewalk there were plastic bags full of trash, and inside almost every bag there was sure to be some tasty treat.

They had an exquisite breakfast.

A man in a stocking cap and a threadbare coat was walking up the street, picking bottles and cans out of the trash. He had often seen the mother dog padding to and from the tank, but this was the first time he had seen the pups accompany her on a search for food.

The man was hungry. He thought about the chicken dinner he would get that afternoon at the Blue Moon Diner, after he turned in his bottles and cans for a nickel

apiece. If all went well, he'd have money left over for a pair of boots that didn't leak.

The mother dog stopped far from the man. She was afraid of people. But the puppies walked closer, and the little girl puppy ventured closest of all.

"Well, good morning, young scout." The man held out the back of his hand for the puppy to sniff. Her nose was about to touch his fingers when a loud, angry voice made everyone stop and look.

"Get outta here, you mutts!" A man charged from his house, swinging a broom over his head. "Look at the mess you've made!" He rushed at the dogs, and the Tank family ran away.

"And that means you, too!" he shouted at the man in the stocking cap, who glared at him for a few seconds and then, shaking his head, turned to follow the dogs.

Down the street and around the corner the dogs ran, right under an eighteen-wheeler parked at the Great Enterprise Trading Company. On they ran . . .

. . . across the Gowanus Canal. The man in the stocking cap, following far behind, saw the long, striped signal arms at both ends of the bridge swing down, letting everyone know that a boat was coming and the drawbridge was about to go up.

At the other end of the bridge stood a man wearing an orange-and-yellow reflective vest. The mother dog ran past him, and the puppies were rushing by when he spoke to them: "Where are you going so fast, you furry rascals?"

The puppies stopped and looked at the man. The boy puppy with the dark, floppy ears trotted along beside him as he closed the steel crash gate. "Well, pup,"

the man said, petting him under the chin, "I think you must like bridge work."

The mother dog watched nervously and made a sound halfway between a whine and a growl.

Just then, the man's partner in the control tower flicked switches and pulled levers to make the bridge go up, so that the oil boat *Gowanus Trader* could pass through.

The man on the deck of the *Gowanus Trader* called to the bridge man, "I see you've got some new helpers."

"Yeah, especially this one," the bridge man called back, patting the puppy with the dark, floppy ears. "He's making sure I do everything right."

The other two puppies started running along the bank beside the *Gowanus Trader*,
and soon the puppy with the dark, floppy ears ran off to join them. The man on the
boat cheered them on.

The mother dog wasn't interested in boats, so she headed back to the tank.

At the end of the canal, the boat docked at the Bayside Oil Company, where another man grabbed the boat's hose and connected it to a big pipe on the dock. The *Gowanus Trader* pumped its cargo of oil into Bayside's underground storage tanks.

The puppy with the pointed ears jumped from the dock onto the boat. "Welcome aboard," said the man on the *Gowanus Trader*. "Maybe someday when you're bigger you can go for a ride with me. But not today." And he put the puppy ashore.

After their adventure on the canal, the puppies trotted toward home. As they passed through the yard of the concrete plant, a driver was washing down the chute of his truck. The girl puppy stopped to drink from a puddle.

"Don't drink that, little dog!" the driver told her. "It's got cement in it, and who knows what else. Tomorrow I'll bring you all a clean bowl of fresh water."

That afternoon at the Blue Moon Diner, the man in the stocking cap was finishing his chicken dinner when the bridge worker and the man from the *Gowanus Trader* walked in. They were talking about the dogs.

While Maggie, the owner of the Blue Moon, cleared away his dishes, the man in the stocking cap told her all about the dogs and the man with the broom.

"Poor dogs," she said. "They have to eat, too."

"I hope they make it through the winter," said the bridge man.

"I wanted to grab that guy's broom," said the man in the stocking cap, moving his arms suddenly and clenching his fists.

"You can grab *that* broom if you want to," Maggie replied, nodding toward the end of the counter.

The man grinned and gulped the last of his coffee. He took the broom and started sweeping at one end of the diner. He didn't mind helping Maggie. She often gave him something to eat even when he couldn't pay for it. Tonight, though, he did have money, and after he'd paid for dinner he had $6.45 left over.

Later, when he lay down to sleep in his cardboard box under the Brooklyn–Queens Expressway, he knew just what he was going to do with the extra money. The boots could wait.

That night, it snowed. Everything was still along the canal, and everyone slept—
except for the little girl puppy.

The man in the stocking cap walked through the new snow toward the Tank family's home, carrying a big, colorful paper bag. Approaching the tank, he opened the bag and tossed great handfuls of dog food to the boy puppies and their mother.

"Where's your sister?" he asked. He got down on his hands and knees and looked inside the tank and saw the puppy. "Is that you, little girl? Are you all right?"
The puppy just lay there and made a small, sad sound. She was very sick.

"Up we go," he said, and he carried her off across the snowy lot, away from her brothers and her worried mother. As they went along, he spoke softly to her, explaining that they were going to get help and that she would be all right. He decided to give her a name. At the beginning of each new block he thought of a name, but by the end of the block he knew that the name wasn't quite right. Block after block, name after name, they went on.

Soon the delicious smell of vegetable soup filled the air. A line of people filed through the door of the Grace Mission Soup Kitchen. It was lunchtime, and he hadn't eaten that morning. He couldn't stop now, but he had found the right name.

Finally they reached the Brooklyn Animal Shelter.

"What happened?" asked the woman behind the desk.

"I don't know," the man answered. "She's not really mine. She lives with her mother and brothers in an old cement tank on the Gowanus Canal."

"I suppose she doesn't have a name, then,"
the woman said.

"Yes, she does," he said. "It's Gracie."

"Come with me," she said.

The woman led them into a small room with a shiny metal table in the middle. "Put her on the table." The woman looked into Gracie's eyes and mouth with a tiny flashlight, and she listened to her heart and lungs with a stethoscope. "She's dehydrated," she said. She offered Gracie some broth in a bowl, but Gracie just lay there.

The woman looked at the man and said, "It's going to cost money to care for Gracie and help her get well again."

"I don't have any money," he said. "But I'll work for you. I'll do anything."

"All right. We're shorthanded right now." Handing him two papers, she said, "I'll need you to fill these out. One is for taxes. The other's an application for adoption, in case you want to take Gracie home when she's better."

He filled out the forms. On the line that asked for his address, he wrote, "380 Hoyt Street," the address of the Blue Moon Diner. He knew he couldn't write "Under the Brooklyn–Queens Expressway," and he knew that Maggie would give him any mail sent to him at the Blue Moon.

For the next three days, he cleaned dog pens and cat cages. He mopped floors and shoveled snow.

Each day, Gracie got a little better. She waited for the man to finish his chores,

and when he came near her pen, her tail wagged so hard that her whole body wiggled. The man thought happily, yet a little sadly, too, about the day when he would take her to his home under the Brooklyn–Queens Expressway. "It's really not much of a home," he told her. "Not a whole lot better than a rusty cement tank."

The day before he was going to take Gracie home, her two brothers were brought into the shelter. "What are they doing here?" he asked the woman angrily. "I've been feeding them every day at the tank, and they were doing just fine."

"You told us Gracie's brothers and mother were living wild," she said. "We sent a man out to get them. The mother was too wild and scared; he couldn't get close

to her. But her puppies are better off here where they'll have food and water and a clean, warm bed. And if they're lucky, someone will adopt them."

Before he left the shelter that afternoon, the man stopped by Gracie's pen. "We've got to find homes for your brothers. If we don't . . ." He hated to think about it. He knew what he had to do.

When the man in the stocking cap arrived at the shelter for his last day of work, the woman said, "I went to 380 Hoyt Street yesterday."

"Why did you go there?" he asked gruffly.

"I suspected that you didn't have a real home, and it's our policy not to place animals with people who don't have suitable housing."

"My place suits me fine, and it will suit Gracie. She'll be snug and safe. She'll have plenty to eat, and I'll make sure she gets her shots."

"I'm sure you'll take good care of Gracie, and I want you to have her. But for that to happen, you have to move to a more normal dwelling."

"If I'd been normal, I never would have known that Gracie was sick, and she'd be dead by now."

"I'm not asking you to be normal. I'm simply asking you to move into a normal apartment."

"I can't afford an apartment."

"I think you can if you keep working here. You're a good worker. I'd like to have you stay. Maggie says there's an apartment available over the Blue Moon."

Without saying anything more, the man went off to see Gracie before starting work.

Late that same afternoon, the bridge man and the boat man arrived at the animal shelter.

"I told you we'd come," the bridge man said to the man in the stocking cap.

The bridge man took the puppy with the dark, floppy ears. He named him Inspector.

The boat man took the puppy with the pointed ears. He named him Captain.

So Inspector lives with the bridge man, and every day he works with him on the bridges along the canal.

Captain lives with the boat man. Every day, they work and ride together on the deck of the *Gowanus Trader*.

Gracie and the man in the stocking cap moved into their new home above the
Blue Moon Diner. Almost every morning, they go to work at the animal shelter.
The puppies' mother still sleeps in the old cement tank, and every day she gets

food and fresh water from the driver at the concrete plant. Lately she's even been letting him pet her.

On special days, everyone gets together down by the canal.

And every night Gracie and the man in the stocking cap are snug and safe at home.